TRAI~~NING TIME~~
HARRISON

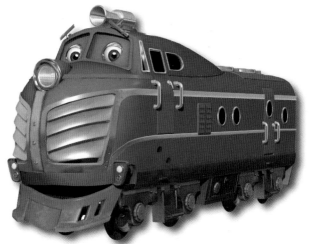

PaRragon

Bath • New York • Singapore • Hong Kong • Cologne • Delhi
Melbourne • Amsterdam • Johannesburg • Auckland • Shenzhen

Vee had a very special announcement.
She needed a chugger to pull the royal carriage.
"I want to do it!" Wilson said excitedly.

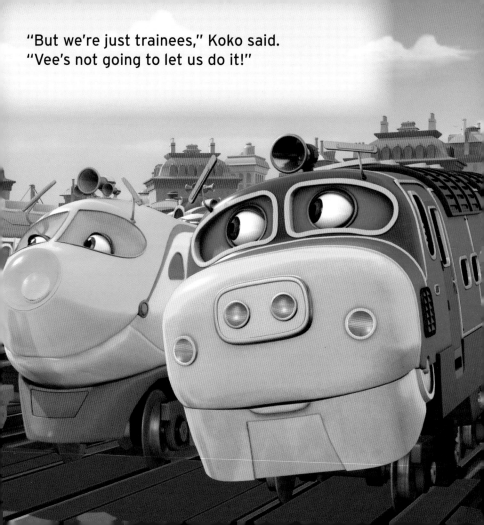

"But we're just trainees," Koko said.
"Vee's not going to let us do it!"

When Harrison heard about the special job, he thought he should be the one pulling the royal carriage. In his rush to get back to the depot, he raced through a red light.

In surprise Olwin jumped off the rails.

"Sorry, Olwin!" Harrison called as he dashed away.

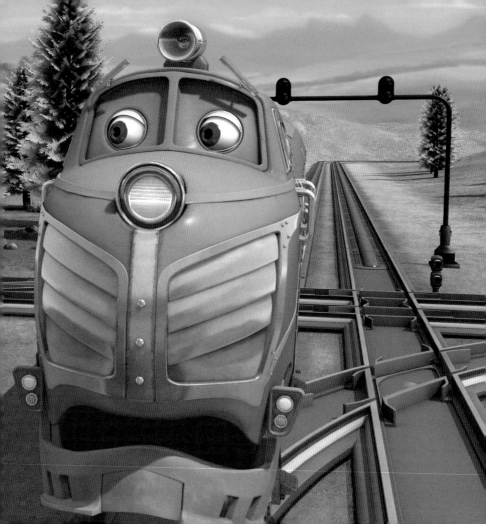

Then Harrison caught up with Chatsworth, who wanted to pull the royal carriage as well.

"The track ahead's blocked!" Harrison cheekily advised. He wanted Chatsworth to turnaround so he could get to the depot first.

"The Prince of Buffertonia is visiting for a royal tour,"
Vee told Harrison when he arrived at the depot.
"Pete will teach you what to do."

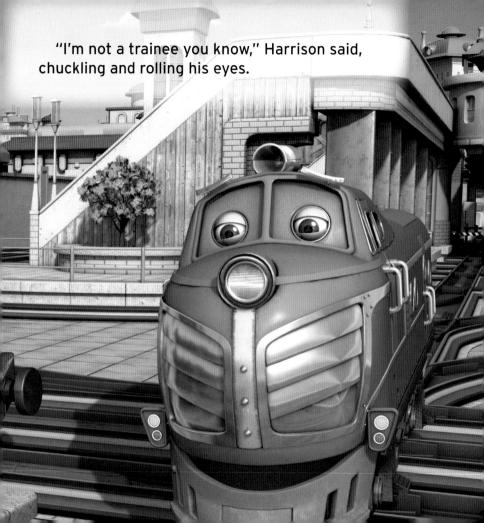

"I'm not a trainee you know," Harrison said, chuckling and rolling his eyes.

Harrison wanted to speed up Pete's practice tour.

"Rattling rivets! Harrison, you're going too fast! The prince won't be able to see anything," Pete puffed.

"Nonsense," Harrison replied, wanting to do the tour his way.

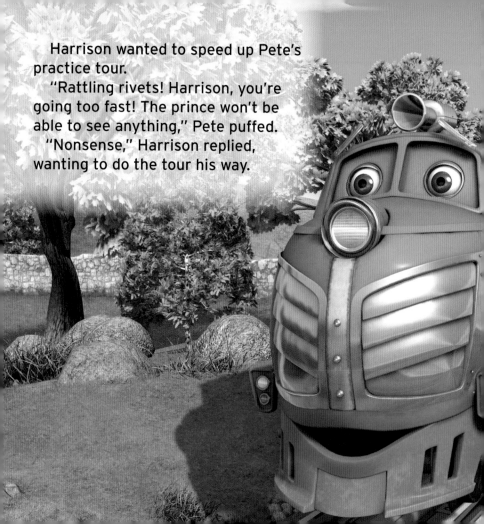

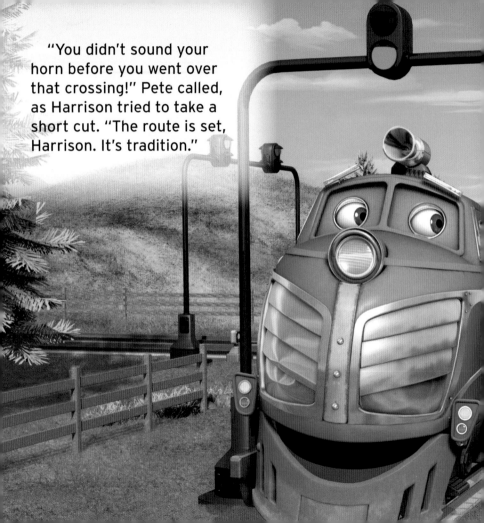

"You didn't sound your horn before you went over that crossing!" Pete called, as Harrison tried to take a short cut. "The route is set, Harrison. It's tradition."

When Vee heard about the practice tour she had an idea.

"I suggest you join the trainees and refresh your memory of the rules of the rails. Off to the training yard, Harrison."

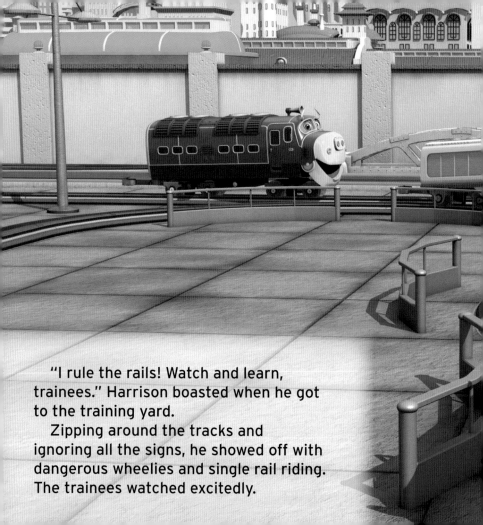

"I rule the rails! Watch and learn, trainees." Harrison boasted when he got to the training yard.

Zipping around the tracks and ignoring all the signs, he showed off with dangerous wheelies and single rail riding. The trainees watched excitedly.

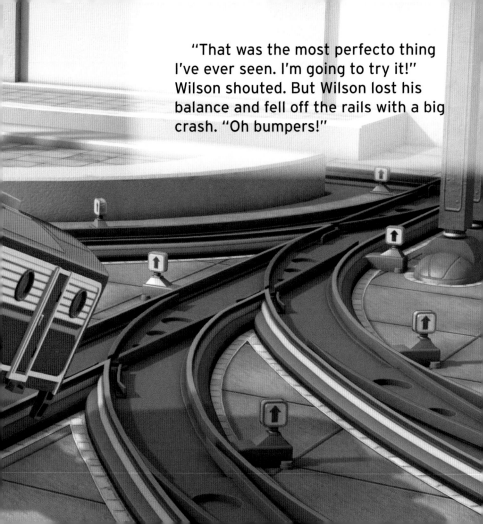

"That was the most perfecto thing I've ever seen. I'm going to try it!" Wilson shouted. But Wilson lost his balance and fell off the rails with a big crash. "Oh bumpers!"

"This is all my fault. I should have set a better example for you," Harrison said, feeling very ashamed as Calley lifted Wilson back onto the rails.

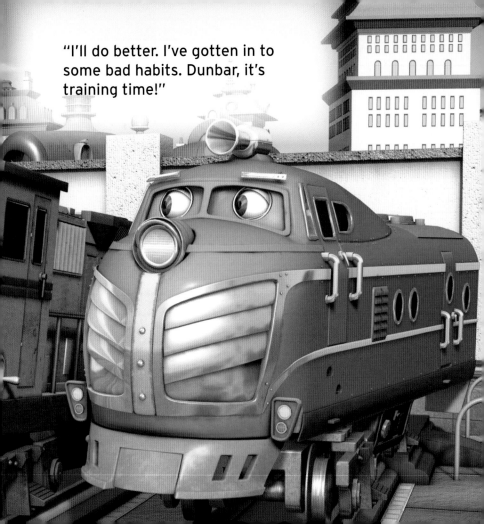

"I'll do better. I've gotten in to some bad habits. Dunbar, it's training time!"

So Harrison practised checking for signs, looking both ways at crossings and riding slow and steady on the tracks.

"Thanks for getting me back on track," he told Wilson.

Everyone watched proudly as Harrison carefully pulled the royal carriage along the rails.

"Go, Harrison, go! Three honks for the prince," Koko called.

"Hurray!" all the watching chuggers cheered.

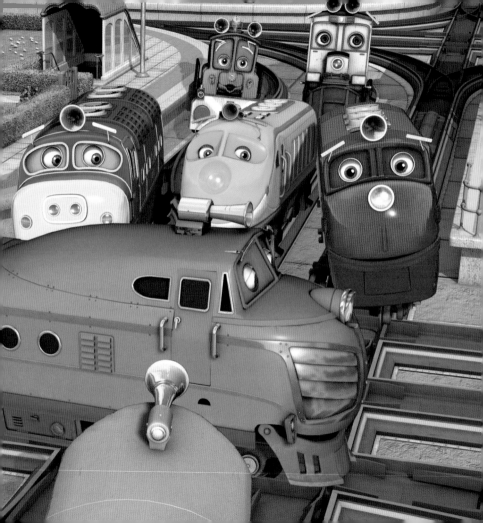

Draw lines to connect each chugger to their matching shadow.

A   B   C   D

1   2   3   4

Answers: A - 4, B - 1, C - 2, D - 3

Can you pick the correct route for Harrison to take the royal tour to Vee?

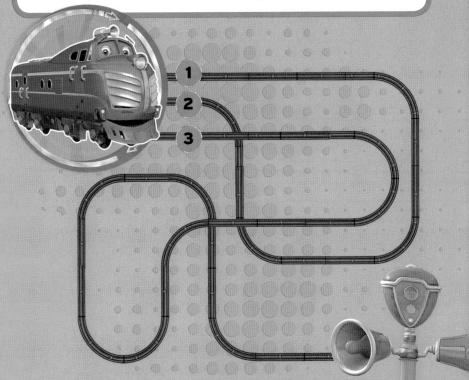

Answer: Route 3

Can you spot five differences between these two pictures from the story? Tick a circle when you spot each difference.

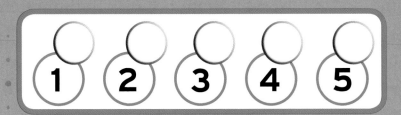

Answers: Calley, Dunbar, the chugger at the front, the royal carriage and the purple gate are missing.

Which picture of Harrison is the odd one out?

A

B

C

D

E

Answer: D

Make your own Harrison!

1. Ask an adult to help you cut out the template carefully with safety scissors.

2. Fold the tabs inwards along the dotted lines.

3. Secure the tabs with glue or sticky tape.

4. Add your stickers to each side.

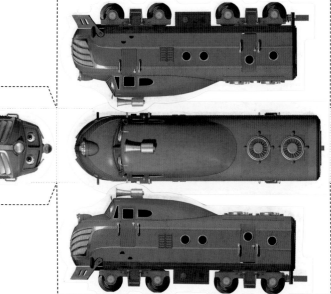

Complete your Chuggington collection.
Tick them off as you collect!

More chuggtastic books to collect!

Stories

ISBN 978-1-4075-6041-0
ISBN 978-1-4075-6042-7
ISBN 978-1-4075-8009-9
ISBN 978-1-4075-8010-4
ISBN 978-1-4075-9530-6
ISBN 978-1-4075-9531-3

Mini stories

ISBN 978-1-4075-9331-9
ISBN 978-1-4075-9332-6
ISBN 978-1-4075-9333-3
ISBN 978-1-4075-9334-0
ISBN 978-1-4075-9335-7
ISBN 978-1-4075-9336-4

Activity books

ISBN 978-1-4075-6126-4
ISBN 978-1-4075-6044-1
ISBN 978-1-4075-6415
ISBN 978-1-4075-8529-0
ISBN 978-1-4075-8422-4

Little library

ISBN 978-1-4075-6043-4

Multi-play books

ISBN 978-1-4075-9882-6
ISBN 978-1-4075-9884-0
ISBN 978-1-84555-437-4

Annual

Activity pack

ISBN 978-1-4075-9885-7

3D books

ISBN 978-1-4075-8349-5
ISBN 978-1-4075-9780-5

Play books

ISBN 978-1-4075-6127-1
ISBN 978-1-4075-8142-2

Story collection

ISBN 978-1-4075-6046-5

Train books

ISBN 978-1-4075-8138-5
ISBN 978-1-4075-8139-2
ISBN 978-1-4075-8140-8